THE HOBBIT™

AN UNEXPECTED JOURNEY

VISUAL COMPANION

Jude Fisher

HarperCollins*Publishers*

Contents

foreword

by martin freeman

For a while, people had told me I should play Bilbo Baggins.

Now, I wasn't really sure how to take this; whether to be pleased that they recognized my sensitivity as an actor, my ability to take on one of the most beloved roles in twentieth-century literature, and carry a huge film by an Oscar-winning team who had already made three of the most popular films in the history of the universe.

Or, did they just mean I had a funny-looking face?

To be honest, I'm still not *quite* sure.

As I write this, about to go and film a scene with some Dwarves and Bard in Laketown, I can honestly say I've had (and am having – there's months to go yet!) the ride of a lifetime. The duration is unlike anything I have known – from arriving in Wellington to finishing final pickups, it will be (should be? may be?) two and a half years. Yup. Pretty long.

Also, the sheer scale that we are working on is awe-inspiring. Every new set that's built, every prop, every piece of costume that we put on, has been so lovingly and skilfully rendered that we actors spend quite a lot of time open-mouthed with admiration. And then there are the locations! It becomes a cliché to go on about New Zealand's natural beauty, but, once you've seen it, you go on about it. It is breathtaking.

At the helm of this ridiculously big ship (but not like the *Titanic*, I must make that quite clear, it is nothing like the *Titanic*) is Peter Jackson. Peter is a man who is fairly familiar with Middle-earth, and he is ably assisted (bossed?) by Fran Walsh and Philippa Boyens, who, between them, know Tolkien like the back of their hand.

Which brings me to the reason why we're all here – a book that was published 75 years ago, which has since become a children's favourite; a quasi-religious work for some, and the daddy of what we know as fantasy fiction. For Benedict Cumberbatch, an actor of indeterminate ability, *The Hobbit* was a part of his boyhood so dear to him that he yearned to play Smaug the Dragon. Which he now is.

For me, it is my privilege to play Bilbo. I hope this wonderful book gives you as much pleasure as *The Hobbit* has to countless others.

Bilbo Baggins

5

Given the chance, hobbits will eat six meals a day. They are very partial to all manner of seedcakes and apple tarts, to pork pies and mince pies, to bread and butter and cream, nuts and honey, chicken and pickle, roast beef and mutton stew, and all sorts of ale, cider, porter and beer. There is nothing a hobbit likes better than to sit around a table laden with delicious delicacies, with friends and family, for food and hospitality are enshrined at the heart of hobbit society. Unless, of course, there is not quite enough to go round...

6

Hobbits

In a quiet corner of the north-west of Middle-earth lies a region of rolling green hills, bright meadows, winding streams, rich farmland and pretty woodlands known as the Shire. Here, in a scatter of villages and hamlets live folk known as hobbits.

Long ago, maybe, they came from the same stock as Men, but these small people, who are around half the height of a full-grown human, have long lived apart from other folk and developed their own society and customs. Shy, retiring, maybe even a little secretive, hobbits like to keep themselves to themselves. They do not travel far from home, or even show much curiosity about the rest of the world: what need is there to go abroad when your home is so pleasant and comfortable?

And like their home, hobbits, too, are generally pleasant and comfortable: especially about the middle, which is, to be honest, rather fat, for hobbits like to eat – a lot. They have shortish legs, a sturdy frame, long brown fingers, slightly pointed ears and brown curly hair, which grows not only on their heads (though rarely on their chins) but also on the tops of their feet. And because the soles of their feet grow thick and leathery, they go barefoot, having no need for shoes and boots.

Hobbits like to dress in the colours of the natural world around them: in grass-green and dandelion-yellow; in the golds and reds of autumn leaves, in sky blue and night-blue. Hobbit men will wear jackets and breeches of velvet and brocade and waistcoats with brass buttons;

the girls choose sprigged cotton dresses with full skirts and petticoats embellished with embroidery and lace, for home crafts flourish in this respectable corner of Middle-earth.

Respectability is much prized in hobbit society. To be well-regarded in this corner of the world it is important to appear sensible, sober and dependable, to be smartly turned out and comfortably off; but equally important that wealth and worldly goods be acquired only by hard work and inheritance and never, EVER, from burglary or going on adventures…

Bilbo Baggins

In the Shire village of Hobbiton, where nothing unexpected ever happens, there lives a hobbit by the name of Bilbo Baggins.

Bilbo is the son of Bungo Baggins and Belladonna Took, and comes from a family (on his mother's side) which has always had something a bit out of the ordinary about it. His ancestor Bullroarer Took was so huge that he was able to ride a full-sized horse rather than a pony. At the Battle of the Green Fields he once charged full tilt into the ranks of the Goblins from the Misty Mountains and knocked their king Golfimbul's head right off with his club. (It flew a hundred yards through the air and fell down a rabbit hole, and that is how the game of golf was invented.)

This sort of behaviour is considered rather too colourful by usual hobbit standards and it has taken quite some time for the family to recover its reputation. At the age of 50, Bilbo is just heading into a comfortable middle age (for hobbits can live to be 130 years old). He lives alone in a hole in the hillside called Bag End, and is generally well thought of in Hobbiton as a sensible and settled sort of chap.

As a youngster he was always running off to search for Elves in the woods and to explore the borders of the Shire. Now that he has outgrown his adventurous youth, surely the last thing in the world he is likely to consider is to go off into the Wild and Beyond with a wizard and a company of thirteen Dwarves…

But beneath that comfortable, sensible-looking exterior there still beats the heart of an adventurer, one to whom adversity and danger, though terrifying, are also a challenge he is ready to meet, with the sort of courage and imagination only Gandalf might expect from him.

Bag End

Bilbo's home is a classic hobbit-hole, set deep into the hillside of Hobbiton. What looks small and modest from the exterior is inside surprisingly spacious and extensive, comprising many rooms joined by a warren of passageways: a sitting room made cosy by a homely hearth; a study stuffed with books and papers; bedrooms and bathrooms; a more than serviceable kitchen; and an extremely well-stocked larder.

Mirroring the rounded nature of their inhabitants, hobbit-holes tend to have circular windows and doors, curved walls and beams, and Bag End is no exception. Much attention has been paid to detail and craftsmanship throughout, where wood has been turned and polished and carved by local artisans skilled in carpentry and cabinet-making. Everywhere you look there is something to be admired, for hobbits set much store by the neatness and prettiness of their homes, as well as their functionality.

Even in the midst of the fiercest storm, the hardest rain or the most howling wind, Bag End will keep its inhabitants safe and warm. It is the sort of place to be remembered with fondness and yearning when home comforts are lacking and you are travelling beyond the Edge of the Wild.

11

Gandalf the Grey

The old codgers who drink in the Green Dragon Inn at Bywater have the habit of referring to Gandalf the Grey as a rogue, a fraud, a vagabond.

The wizard in question is certainly a wanderer, turning up in various quarters of Middle-earth at the most unexpected times. The folk of Hobbiton think he is simply a teller of tales about dragons, the rescue of princesses and the unlikely luck of widows' sons, an expert with fireworks and other small benevolent spells conjured for the delight of children. But there is so much more than meets the eye to this tall, dignified figure in his tall, pointed hat, long grey cloak, silver scarf and long white beard.

Gandalf the Grey is no mere conjurer, but a member of the Istari – the brotherhood of wizards – and as such is a wielder of powerful magic and is more knowledgeable of the history and peoples of Middle-earth than almost any other in the world.

Contrary to appearances, his wanderings are never random. Underneath those straggling grey brows are a pair of very sharp eyes, always assessing the state of the world, always on the lookout for any sign that there is a resurgence of the dark powers that have lain dormant these many years. And indeed that is why he has come to Hobbiton, bringing with him Thorin Oakenshield and The Company of Dwarves.

Of all the group, Gandalf is the one who best knows the dangers The Company is likely to face. It is a mark of the importance of The Quest that he would be prepared to risk the safety not only of the Dwarves, but also of young Bilbo Baggins. For of all the peoples of Middle-earth, it is the hobbits for whom Gandalf feels the greatest affection. They represent for him something vital and unspoiled in the world, and such qualities are rare nowadays.

As The Company journeys through the Trollshaw Forest, Gandalf will discover a wonderful weapon, encased in a smooth ivory scabbard. The sword may have been found in a Trolls' cave but it is certainly not Troll-made, being an ancient sword forged by the High Elves of the West, and once wielded by a king of Gondolin during the Goblin-wars. Its name in the Elven tongue is Glamdring, which means 'foe-hammer'. But the Goblins call it Beater, as well they may...

Dwarves

Dwarves are an ancient people who came into being before the existence (it is said) of the Sun and Moon. They speak a secret language known as Khuzdul, which is written in Cirth, an angular runic alphabet developed by the Elves.

Though shorter and stouter than Elves or Men (yet somewhat taller than hobbits), Dwarves are extremely strong for their size, and are fearsome and capable warriors. Dwarves who survive battle can live for as long as 250 years. They wear their hair and beards long and like to plait and braid both in the most elaborate and outlandish fashion. Since both male and female Dwarves grow beards, it can be hard for outsiders to tell them apart.

Dwarves have a great love of beautiful things made by hands and by magic, and a fierce desire for gold and treasure (as well as a keen understanding of the value of such things). They are skilled miners, and will delve deep into the roots of mountains beneath the caverns in which they make their home in search of gold and silver, precious stones and legendary *mithril*, a silver metal beyond price. Their smiths, metalworkers and stonemasons are famed throughout Middle-earth.

Of old the Dwarves forged relationships with Men and Elves, and their goat-drawn carts were to be seen on all the major trading routes of Middle-earth, carrying tools, weapons, armour and metals out of their mountain kingdoms and returning with all those supplies they could not grow underground. But the Dwarves have fallen on hard times, having been dispossessed of their ancestral kingdoms in Khazad-dûm and Erebor, driven out of the first by a monstrous Balrog and the second by the greatest dragon of his day, Smaug the Terrible.

Now, homeless and embittered against those who did not help them in their hour of need, they wander Middle-earth with a grudge in their hearts, and the determined desire to regain their lost homeland.

Thorin Oakenshield

Thorin Oakenshield is the direct descendant of Durin, royal ancestor of all Dwarves; but he is also the scion of a line of kings who have lost their kingdom, a king in exile: but one who fully intends to change his fortune.

His grandfather, Thrór, ruled the great Dwarf-kingdom in Erebor, the Lonely Mountain, near the eastern edge of Mirkwood Forest. But word had spread of the kingdom's wealth, and Smaug the Terrible, a young and hungry fire-drake, blazed down from the north and attacked Erebor, bringing death and devastation with his searing flames. Out of the mountain, by a secret door, fled King Thrór, his son Thráin and a few survivors. They fled south as refugees, and ever since they have been doomed to wander, the dream of their homeland kept alive only in songs and tales.

Thorin is the son of Thráin, and for long years since his father vanished in the dark halls of Khazad-dûm he has borne the heavy burden of the hopes of his people: the dream of one day reclaiming the Lonely Mountain and returning to their home. He is driven by his oath to bring vengeance upon the dragon Smaug; and by the determination to regain the lost treasure of the Dwarves. As king-in-exile he is accompanied by twelve brave companions, including his sister-sons, Fili and Kili for whom, as their guardian, he bears a special responsibility.

His burdens, and the fury that burns within him, have rendered Thorin Oakenshield grim and stern. Broad-shouldered, black of hair and cloak and with a fierce regard and a deep mind, he has a powerful, forbidding presence. When he was younger, Thorin used a piece of oak tree as his shield in battle and from this he earned his name. He wields a pair of great battle-axes; but he is soon to come by an even more fearsome weapon.

In a cave in the Trollshaw Forest, Thorin will find a great Elvish blade
with a squared pattern of diamonds in the head of its pommel, and a line
of runes swirling down into the fuller of the blade. Its name is Orcrist,
which means in the Elvish language 'Goblin-cleaver'.
The Goblins call it simply, Biter.

Fili & Kili

After Ori, by far the youngest Dwarves in The Company of Thorin Oakenshield, are Fili and Kili, the sons of his sister, Dis, daughter of Thráin.

Fili is the older of the two by five years, and he has been charged by his stern uncle to keep a watching eye over his exuberant younger brother, Kili. Since Thorin has no offspring of his own, Fili and Kili are next in line to the Dwarvish throne, albeit that the kingdom they stand to inherit is currently occupied by a fearsome dragon. Never having seen action, they are keen to go into battle to win back their ancestral lands.

Despite his grim appearance, Thorin is regarded by the pair as a father-figure. For most of their lives he has stood in place of their dead father as a guardian and they are fiercely loyal to him as their king. The two young Dwarves are intensely proud of their royal blood, although Fili, as the elder brother, feels the responsibility of being the next in line more heavily than the irrepressible Kili.

Energetic and good-humoured, the pair have the sharpest eyes and the quickest feet in The Company: they are the lookouts, scouts and hunters of the group, always ready to run ahead to spy out the lie of the land or to chase down a rabbit. From an early age they have both been given intensive weapons training, making them swift and able fighters.

Kili is tall for a Dwarf, and is both inquisitive and spirited, with a rebellious streak and a twinkle in his eye that can land him in trouble. However, beneath his irreverent exterior lies the serious desire to prove himself worthy of his illustrious bloodline and to win praise from his royal uncle, of whom he is somewhat in awe.

Fili and Kili fight together as a team: their brotherly bond is extremely strong. They each carry an arsenal of lethal weapons: Fili has a war-hammer, several throwing axes and a pair of razor-sharp swords; his brother, in addition to his knives and short axes, also carries a bow, with which he is a deadly shot.

Map
of
Middle-earth

Far over the Misty Mountains cold,

To dungeons deep and caverns old,

The pines were roaring on the height,

The winds were moaning in the night,

The fire was red, it flaming spread,

The trees like torches blazed with light.

Balin

The Dwarf-lord Balin and his younger brother, Dwalin, the sons of Fundin, are, like Thorin and his nephews, also of Durin's royal line.

Balin is the most venerable Dwarf of The Company, rumoured to be 178 years of age at the beginning of the quest. He is recognizable by his long white beard and moustache. Despite his advanced years, his eyes are still sharp and, though by nature gentle and wise, he is a skilled and powerful warrior. Forced to live a life fraught with war and the struggle to survive, he endured many battles; he carries the scars upon him, and on the notched blade of his mighty sword.

Balin was there at the Front Gate of the Lonely Mountain with King Thráin and the young prince Thorin when Smaug descended in flame and fire, and he saw the town of Dale destroyed. He also accompanied Thráin on the doomed expedition to regain the kingdom of Khazad-dûm, when his king was captured by Goblins and lost to his people.

Since then, Balin has been like a father to Thorin Oakenshield, and is the one Thorin turns to first for advice and support in times of doubt. And as the elder statesman of the group, he often acts as the second in command and drafter of official contracts.

But having seen their kingdom lost to the dragon, he knows how terrible the enemy is; of all The Company he harbours troubling doubts about the wisdom of a return to Erebor.

Dwalin

Younger brother to Balin and another of the senior members of The Company is Dwalin. He and Thorin Oakenshield grew up as childhood friends, though he is some years older than the king-in-waiting. Together they have shared the bitter travails of exile, and plenty of hard action, having fought their way through innumerable Goblins and Orcs. Through it all, he remains Thorin's staunchest supporter and maintains an unshakeable belief in his friend's leadership.

Dwalin has developed a ritual of memorializing every significant episode in his life with a new tattoo – on his arms and hands, and even across his scalp. As a veteran fighter, he has amassed a truly impressive collection, many of the designs taking the form of ancient Dwarvish runes.

As befits such a fierce warrior, Dwalin is heavily armed. He bears an enormous war-hammer, and a pair of brutal knuckle-dusters. He also wields a pair of wickedly sharp war-axes, which he carries crossed upon his back (along with a monstrously heavy pack).

Although his weapons are utilitarian rather than decorative, he has named his axes, calling the one 'Grasper' and the other 'Keeper': for the first axe will grasp the soul of an opponent, while the second will keep it. He takes great care of his weapons, since his life depends on them, and they have saved both his life and the lives of his companions many times, as the many scars on the blades can testify. He cherishes every nick and scratch, since each marks the death of an enemy.

Dwalin does not suffer fools gladly, nor is he the most loquacious member of The Company, leaving the talking to his brother, Balin. In truth, Dwalin prefers his weapons to do the talking for him, and he is looking forward to letting them chatter loudly…

33

Bifur

Bifur and his cousins Bofur and Bombur are some of the few in The Quest for the Lonely Mountain who are not descended from the line of Durin. No royal blood here: these Dwarves are raised from among the coal miners and the iron-workers of the West of Middle-earth, and as such they carry weapons which reflect their heritage – mattocks and picks and other workmanlike tools.

Bifur is the odd one out of the group: a loner, rather strange. He mumbles, grunts and mutters in Khuzdul, an antique version of the secret language of the Dwarves, but no one apart from the wizard Gandalf can understand a word of what he says.

What has made him this way is the axe-wound to his skull, still clearly visible since the axe-head is still firmly embedded there. Now he is looking for the Orc who put it there, and when he finds him…

In a fight, he goes wild, laying about himself in furious abandon with his great boar-spear and his knives; or even with his fists and head if he is ever rendered weaponless.

But even in the midst of battle there are moments when he will come to a complete standstill and gaze around, lost and bewildered, no doubt wondering how his life has come to this pass from his rather more genteel origins.

34

Despite the heavy tools they are used to working with, Bifur, Bofur and Bombur are equally skilled with a delicate whittling knife. They help to finance The Company as it makes its way towards the Lonely Mountain by making and selling clever little wooden toys. Bifur's toys are rather disturbing, sometimes even monstrous. But children seem to love them anyway.

Bofur

Talkative, energetic and wildly optimistic, Bofur likes to take a leading role whenever he can, and if there is trouble to be got into, then Bofur will be right there, especially if there is beer or music involved. (He has a fine singing voice and has been known to play the flute.)

He maintains a feisty relationship with his brother, Bombur, teasing him mercilessly about his vast size, his slowness and shyness, and his poor sibling is often the target of his sharp tongue (or the sole of his boot).

He enjoys injecting a dramatic edge into any situation, and is often guilty of exaggerating (as he believes) the dangers that the members of The Quest are likely to face, in order to tease his companions. What he does not realize is that his exaggerations barely do justice to the real perils that await The Company.

But beneath the wicked sense of humour (which lightens the mood in the darkest of moments) lies a tough scrapper, fiercely loyal to his family, his companions and his king. His weapon of choice, true to his family's mining background, is a great mattock.

Not the bravest of the Dwarves, nor a trained warrior, Bofur joined the quest to seek his fortune; and also (rumour has it) because he was told the beer was free…

Bombur

Enormously fat, even for a Dwarf, and with his fiery red beard plaited into an impressive hoop, Bombur is unmistakeable. He hardly speaks (perhaps because his brother Bofur speaks quite enough for both of them), and tends to be quiet and thoughtful, much given to musings about where his next meal may be coming from.

But for all his size, Bombur is not driven by simple greed and undiscriminating appetite. This Dwarf has a love of the finer things in life and has developed into something of a fussy cook (though his companions might not always agree), a function he carries out for the whole Company.

As a result of this self-imposed employment, Bombur is armed with cooking implements: a vast ladle, pots and pans (all excellent for braining Goblins with), and a very large, sharp roasting fork. None of which he is afraid to use; for, true to his roots, like all Dwarves, Bombur is a doughty and determined warrior in battle.

36

Dori

Dori, Nori and Ori are brothers, although they are as unlike one another as bats and bacon. Dori is the eldest of the three and fancies himself as something of a sophisticate. After all, his family is related to that of Thorin Oakenshield, albeit 'on the wrong side of the blanket', as Dori says cryptically. He is unwilling to explain exactly what he means by this.

He has a preference for the finer things in life: good ales, vintage cheese and well-crafted weaponry, and his clothing is always made from the best quality cloth. He wears his hair braided and his beard – a long one, as befits his age and status – enclosed in a fine, engraved-silver beard-case.

His own upbringing having been strict and moral, he is well-versed in good manners and proper behaviour, and tends to be over-protective of his little brother, Ori, and somewhat disapproving of their middle brother, Nori (for good reason).

The other Dwarves regard Dori as something of an old fusspot (and a hypochondriac): but they certainly appreciate his abilities in a fight. Cross him at your peril. For all his genteel ways, Dori is very handy not only with a sword but also with his trusty bolas, which have cracked a good many Goblin heads in their day.

Nori

Nori is the middle brother of the three, but on the surface at least he appears to have little in common with either of them.

Nori is a crafty, evasive character who does not much like talking about himself. He admits to once being a miner, but if pressed will add that he left home at an early age. (He tells you this with a gleam in his eye; but will not elaborate.) Since then he has lived a nomadic life, living off the land and off his wits. He's an expert hunter and forager, of necessity, and is therefore a very useful Dwarf to have on such an expedition. Although there can be times when foraging crosses a line, and becomes theft…

It is not without reason that Dori keeps a close eye on Nori and ensures that he does not become too bad an influence on young Ori.

As he has been out of the bosom of his family for many, many years, Nori sees The Quest as an opportunity to reacquaint himself with his brothers. Of course, if a little booty were to come his way during the course of the expedition he wouldn't be unhappy.

Nori carries with him a wide variety of weaponry that he has come upon, or purloined; including a staff, daggers and a wickedly sharp fleshing knife. Not always the fairest in a fight (he has been known to stab an opponent in the back), Nori has been in a number of brawls in his time and certainly knows how to look after himself. But now he is determined to look after young Ori too; and although he may not always see eye to eye with older brother Dori, Dwarf-blood is thicker than water and anyone who threatens Nori or either of his brothers had better beware.

Ori

Ori is the youngest and least experienced of all of The Company of Thorin Oakenshield; a gentle, sweet-natured Dwarf who has never travelled anywhere before, and never seen a Goblin let alone a terrifying dragon (except maybe in books). He is certainly the least prepared (apart from, maybe, Bilbo Baggins) for such a dangerous mission. And indeed, to look at him you might think he had just wandered out into the countryside on a slightly chilly day to sketch birds or flowers; for he hardly looks equipped to set out on such a dangerous journey, dressed as he is in scarf, cap and mittens, all badly knitted by his mother, and carrying his satchel.

But if any of the dark, disturbing details he has heard from the rest of the group about dragons, Wargs or Trolls frighten him, he is determined not to show it or to allow them to dismay him. Ori turns an ever-optimistic, brave face to the world and is something of a talisman to the entire Company, all of whom are protective of the young Dwarf.

He looks upon some of the other Dwarves (particularly his king-in-exile, Thorin Oakenshield) with great respect and not a little awe, part of which may be because they all seem to have better weapons than he does, and know how to use them. Poor Ori has been vouchsafed only a little knife and a catapult, although he refuses to let this hold him back when it comes to the sticking point.

And he has other skills: Ori is the scribe of the group. The satchel he carries with him contains his quills and inks, and his journal, in which he records his impressions of the journey, and makes sketches. One day, without doubt, this book will turn out to be a most fascinating artefact.

Oin

Oin and Gloin are the sons of Gróin, and being most expert in the use of tinder and flints, even in the most trying of circumstances, are the acknowledged fire-lighters of The Company.

Extremely canny with money, Oin has come on the quest not only to support his kin (he and Gloin are distant cousins of Thorin Oakenshield) but also because he has a substantial sum of money invested in the venture.

Erudite and well-read, Oin is also the healer of the group and carries with him a considerable collection of plants and herbal remedies. For this reason, the others often refer to him as 'the Apothecary'. He has the ability to make all manner of herbal salves to speed the healing of wounds, which may come in very useful on this journey. It is said that the word 'ointment' derives from their maker. He has also acted as a midwife on those rare occasions on which Dwarf-children are born. It is rumoured that he was present to deliver Gimli, Gloin's son, and that he dropped the baby on his head, which explains a great deal.

A bit deaf now in his advanced years (for he is 167 years old) he uses an ear-trumpet to aid his hearing, but unfortunately it is not always very effective, and misunderstandings can occur. Quite often.

Despite his venerable age, he can still lay about him to brutal effect with his iron-shod staff, and he has picked up many a cunning fighting trick in his time, and forgotten many more.

Gloin

Gloin is one of The Company's elder statesmen and is also their spokesman. He considers himself something of a diplomat, but in fact is extremely outspoken, even pugnaciously opinionated.

He is also, it must be said, extremely mean with money. Dwarves are, as a race, very aware of the value of all things, right down to the smallest coin, but Gloin takes this trait and renders it an art form. As a result, he is the perfect choice as The Company's treasurer, a responsibility he takes very seriously indeed. He carries with him at all times a finely crafted abacus, each bead of which is carved with Dwarvish runes, and by means of this tallies up the group's finances, their revenues (from toy-making and -selling) and their outgoings. Perhaps it is partly because of these preoccupations that Gloin is suspicious of everyone and everything (but particularly Elves and wizards).

He is one of few Dwarves who is married and has offspring. He has a fine young son, Gimli who, at the age of only 62, is regarded as far too young to be gadding about on a dangerous quest. However, he carries a portrait of his young son and his wife – an acclaimed beauty with a fine beard – with him at all times.

The massive battle-axe he carries was inherited from his father, Gróin; and one day it will be handed on to his own son.

The Quest

Far away to the east of Middle-earth, across the Edge of the Wild, over the Misty Mountains, through Wilderland, across the Great River Anduin, beyond the vast forest of Mirkwood, stands a solitary peak amid a scene of utmost devastation.

Its name is Erebor, the Lonely Mountain, and once it was a rich kingdom in which gold and treasure was piled high: the pride of the Dwarves, the embodiment of their honour and well-being. But then came the dragon Smaug, out of the north, to drive the Dwarves from their mountain kingdom and incinerate those who would not run. The moon was blotted out by smoke from the dragon's fire. The memory of that terrifying day and night is burned into the memory of all who witnessed it, like the young prince Thorin Oakenshield and his companions Balin and Dwalin, who escaped the fate of their compatriots by means of a secret door out of the mountain.

Since that time, all those years ago, the dragon has not left his lair except to hunt, and the Dwarves have been exiled: forced to wander from town to town in humiliation, scratching out a living by whatever means they can. But lately it is rumoured that Smaug has not been seen abroad for some time. Which may mean that the treasure the Dwarves of Erebor amassed with such industry now lies unguarded, prey to the greed of any who might look to the mountain with covetous eyes.

And so Thorin and Gandalf have formed The Company, to journey across Middle-earth to the Lonely Mountain, there to determine whether or not the dragon has abandoned the halls of Erebor. Gandalf has his own reasons for The Quest; but the stubbornness of Dwarves is legendary, and the idea of unguarded treasure has kindled a fire in their hearts, the sort of fire only a Dwarf may feel. Moreover, Thorin has sworn a solemn oath to take back his kingdom and save the honour of his people.

They have a map, made by Thorin's grandfather, Thrór; and a large silver key to the secret door, entrusted to Gandalf against just such an opportunity. But The Company also needs someone with stealth and courage who may creep through the tunnels unseen and undetected, someone unknown to the dragon and who will not be distracted by all that gold. And this is why The Company has travelled all the way to Hobbiton to roust poor Bilbo Baggins out of his comfortable existence; for Gandalf has promised the Dwarves that Bilbo is a very accomplished and enterprising burglar! Such a suggestion is outrageous to such a respectable young hobbit; but Bilbo's journey into the Wild is an experience that is about to change him for life and bring into play qualities he never knew he possessed.

It is a dangerous venture, but also possibly a very lucrative undertaking: and where risk and profit are involved, a contract must be signed.

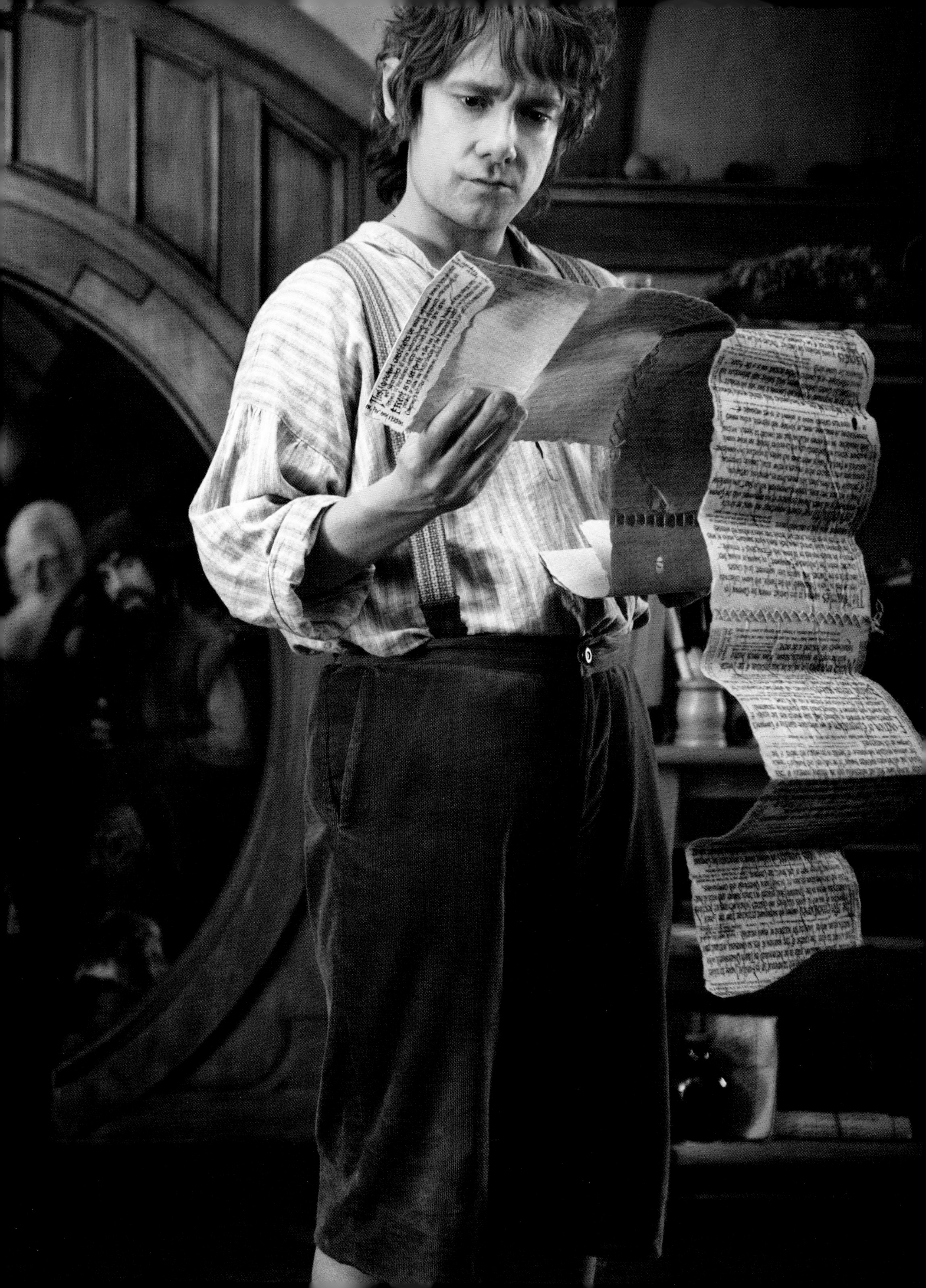

Trollshaw Forest

The Trollshaw Forest is to be found in the Lone-lands far to the east of the Shire, on the other side of the Weather Hills at the Edge of the Wild; this is a boggy, grim, boulder-strewn place at the best of times, but made all the more bleak and miserable when it is pouring with rain. The forest itself is tangled and forbidding: not the sort of place to enter in the dark. But when shelter is needed, in which to make camp and to cook the rabbits that Fili and Kili will (with some luck) bring back from their hunting expedition, beggars cannot be choosers.

It is the sort of place where ponies may go missing, and where chancy lights may be spied through the trees: the sort of place, in other words, that will make you think fondly of a cosy little hobbit-hole all those long days and miles behind you to the west, where a proper fire crackles in the hearth, where the pantry is full of all sorts of good food that does not come with heads and fur attached, and where a comfortable bed, with a feather mattress and warm covers, beckons once you have eaten your fill.

It is also the sort of place where Trolls may be found…

Trolls

Tom, Bert and William are mountain trolls from the Ettenmoors who have taken up residence in the Trollshaw Forest because they have found good pickings may be had there. Despite being slow-witted, thick-skinned and lumbering creatures, they live off the unwitting people and unlucky animals that cross their path, and by pillaging any farms in the area of sheep, cows, chickens and farmers (though the farmers in the Trollshaw Forest are a tough breed, and taste positively leathery).

Trolls are always active at night because they cannot go about their business by day (sunlight is very dangerous to them). So they always make sure they have a nice big cave into which they can retreat before the first rays of dawn, where they can sleep and guard all the treasure they have gathered from robbing the corpses of their victims, and other places.

Rivendell

As The Company approaches the edge of the Wild they pass through a silent wasteland leading towards the distant Misty Mountains. Following a narrow track marked by white stones, they come upon sudden ravines and chasms through which waterfalls cascade. Pine woods tower on either side as the path zigzags sharply back and forth on its precipitous descent into a hidden valley – the Valley of Imladris. At the bottom of the track a narrow stone bridge spans the tumbling river. One by one the ponies must trek across bearing Thorin and Company and their packs; and at last, on midsummer's eve, they will reach Rivendell, the Last Homely House east of the Sea.

This Elven refuge has stood, safely hidden from the outside world, for thousands of years, protected by the magic of its lord, Elrond the Halfelven. Within are wonders: gardens, courtyards, sunlit terraces and buildings so beautiful that all who see them are filled with awe and delight. Full of light and warmth and comfort, tapestries, statues and carvings, Rivendell is a perfect place in which to rest, to think, to talk and to plan: for no evil thing can enter there.

Elves

The most ancient of all the peoples of Middle-earth are the Elves. Graceful, tall and slender, with ears as pointed as a leaf and eyes as keen as an eagle's, they walk lightly upon the earth. Their voices, in speech or in melody, are a joy to hear.

Some Elves may be dark-haired and grey-eyed, like Elrond, the Master of Rivendell. Others may be silver of hair, but most, including the Elves of the Greenwood and Lothlorien, who have never passed west of the Misty Mountains, are golden-haired. Some among the Silvan Elves may tend towards a more russet colouring, in keeping with their surroundings.

It is said that Elves endure only as long as Middle-earth endures. Indeed, no elf has ever died of natural ageing, unlike the other peoples of the world, although like anyone else they may be killed by violence or by accident. And thus, immortal and ageless, they make their lives in Middle-earth until they no longer have the wish to do so. Then they may decide to travel over the Sea to the Undying Lands in the far west, where they can continue to exist in a state of bliss, away from the strife and cares of the mortal world.

Given such longevity, the Elves are the lore-keepers and historians of Middle-earth and some are as learned and wise as even the Istari wizards.

Elves have a great love of beauty and in times of peace have given rein to their soaring imaginations to create the most beautiful art, sculpture, tapestries and architecture – all the finest of things that can be made with a pure heart and soul and hand. They are also wonderful poets and song-makers, and the sound of Elves singing casts an enchantment on all who hear. Their songs echo down the ages.

It is not only things of beauty that the Elves have created, but also artefacts of immense power. It was the Elves who wrought the Rings of Power, forged by the Dwarves but imbued with the Elves' most potent magic. But in times of unrest they will harden their hearts; long ago they forged such deadly weapons as the swords The Company find in the Trolls' cave: Orcrist, the Goblin-cleaver; Glamdring the 'foe-hammer' and Bilbo Baggins' sword, which being an Elven blade glows blue in the presence of Goblins and Orcs. For of all their many enemies in the world, the Elves are their fiercest, most dangerous foe. As the guardians of Middle-earth, of its beauty and its light, the Elves are the enemy of those who seek to bring darkness and ruination to the world.

The White Council

Something evil is stirring in Middle-earth, so the most powerful Elves and wizards arrange to gather in the safe haven of Rivendell to discuss their concerns. Amongst them are Elrond, the Master of Rivendell, Galadriel, the Lady of Lothlorien, Gandalf the Grey, a member of the order of wizards known as the Istari, and his superior, Saruman the White, the greatest of the Istari wizards, who has travelled to the council meeting from the iron tower of Orthanc at Isengard.

Saruman is a master of lore and magic; but his great knowledge has made him arrogant and sometimes wilfully blind to the growing power of others. Neither does he care for the small folk of the world, and is dismissive of any opinions not his own. As far as he is concerned, the Watchful Peace that has endured for the past four hundred years still holds.

But Gandalf has travelled widely through Middle-earth, keeping both his eyes and ears open, and by such simple means has become aware of the many signs of evil – great and small – that are beginning to make their presence felt in the world. There is of course the matter of Smaug the dragon; a danger in his own right, but a terrifying prospect if in alliance with darker powers. There has also been a resurgence of Orcs and Wargs, and Trolls have come down out of the mountains to raid farms and villages: the roads are no longer safe for travellers. Others speak of a sickness in the place once known as Greenwood the Great, now called by many of the woodmen who work there Mirkwood.

Worst of all, there are signs that something evil, perhaps even with the power to raise the dead, has taken up residence in the ruined fortress of Dol Guldur.

And then there is the matter of the missing Ring of Power, lost long, long ago…

Galadriel

The Lady Galadriel is ruler, with her husband Celeborn, of the Elven kingdom of Lothlorien.

Lothlorien, or the Golden Wood, was made a safe refuge for the Wood-Elves by Galadriel during the Third Age, somewhere the evil forces of the world could not penetrate. In Lothlorien are to be found the towering mallorn trees, the tallest and loveliest trees in Middle-earth. Because her daughter Celebrian is married to Elrond Halfelven, Galadriel retains close contact with Rivendell; less so with the Elves of the Greenwood.

She is a striking figure, with her luminous white skin and her flowing golden hair. Although she looks fragile and ethereal, appearances are deceptive, for she is the mightiest of all the Elves who remain in Middle-earth and is possessed with the gift of foresight. She wears Nenya, the Ring of Adamant, or the Ring of Water, one of the three great Elven Rings of Power, and armed with this Galadriel may be a match for even the worst evil that walks abroad.

And like Gandalf the Grey, her natural ally, she is well aware that the dark powers never sleep and that it is only through constant vigilance that the world may be kept safe.

60

elrond

The Master of Rivendell is Elrond, a wise and ancient lord who is thousands of years old and one of the great powers left in Middle-earth.

He is known as 'Halfelven' because his lineage can be traced all the way back to the ancient hero Beren, a mortal man who fell in love with the Elven princess Lúthien, who gave up her immortality for him; but it is also said that his ancestors were the angelic Maiar who entered Middle-earth at the beginning of time.

Long ago, Elrond fought in the Elven army against the Dark Lord Sauron in the Second Age of Middle-earth, so he knows well the nature and strength of evil and does not underestimate it. He wears Vilya, the sapphire Ring of Air, the most powerful of the three Elven Rings of Power.

Gollum

Down in the roots of the Misty Mountains, in the labyrinth of caverns, lakes and streams that lie in the gloom dwells a small, sinister being. This creature is pale-skinned but with a heart as dark as darkness itself, and two big round pale eyes, eyes that have adapted over the course of the five hundred years in which it has lived down there to shine like great green lamps. Living in the dark has also made the creature's sense of hearing and smell equally acute. Anything that strays down there under the mountains will be sensed by this diminutive predator and, most likely, eaten.

The creature's name is Gollum, for the horrible swallowing noise he makes in his throat. His home is a small slimy island in the middle of a deep, deadly cold lake. He spends much of his time rowing quietly around the lake in a little coracle, paddling it with his feet, but never making a ripple so as not to disturb his prey: the blind grey fish he grabs up as quick as thought. However, he is not averse to making a meal of anything else that comes his way…

Once, a long, long time ago, though it is hard to believe it, Gollum was not unlike a hobbit and his name was Sméagol. The horrible transformation that has come over him is the result of the influence of the object he refers to as his 'birthday present', a certain golden ring that came into his possession during a fishing trip with his friend Déagol.

Poor Déagol did not survive that fishing trip. It could be said that Sméagol did not either, for the creature he has become bears little resemblance to the hobbit he once was.

The Ring

Long, long ago nineteen Great Rings were forged, each one imbuing its bearer with magical powers and longevity. The Elven kings held three of these Rings and seven were owned by the Dwarf-lords. The kings of Men held nine. Treacherously, a single ruling Ring was forged by Sauron, the Dark Lord of Mordor, in order to gain dominion over the rest and in this Ring he invested much of his own power. When that Ring was lost to him, the Dark Lord was therefore much diminished.

By many curious and roundabout means, the Ruling Ring found its way into the possession of Gollum, who guards it with a jealous fervour.

Once worn, the Ring makes its magical presence felt, for it confers invisibility on whoever wears it; but it also channels dark whispers into the mind. Its influence being both powerful and malign, the Ring will always corrupt its wearer, unless they are immensely strong of both mind and spirit. But Gollum was one of the Riverfolk and not so very different from Bilbo once – but now he is barely more than a shadow of the Ring itself. To lose it will diminish him even further … so when he cannot find it, he feels its loss keenly…

Goblins

Gollum is not the only one to make his home inside the Misty Mountains. Down here, in the dark tunnels and caves that pit the rock underlying the snow-capped peaks, dwells a race of monstrous creatures. Sly and malicious, ugly and disease-ridden, they avoid the light of day, for it makes their legs wobble and their heads dizzy. As a result, their skin is afflicted with sores, their bones deformed; they are shorter than Men, sometimes even as small as hobbits. But for all this they are wiry and strong, keen of nose and sharp of tooth and claw, and always to be feared. They are the Goblins.

Down beneath the High Pass of the Misty Mountains they have created a bizarre shanty town, cobbled together out of scavenged items used in odd ways. Skulls and skeletons and horns and human implements are combined with more conventional building materials to make weird, rickety structures and ugly, scaffolded dwellings, strangely furnished with all manner of peculiar items put to uses for which they were never designed.

Goblins make nothing of beauty themselves, but they are very adept at making clever artifices — weapons, instruments of torture, curious engines and devices — anything, in fact, for doing harm to others.

The Goblin King

Their king is the most hideous of all, twice the size of every other Goblin, with a throat that billows in and out like that of a bullfrog, the air whistling through holes in his rancid skin. When he sings, as he often does, his voice echoes throughout the tunnels and caverns of Goblin Town, carrying his presence to every dark corner of his kingdom. He is a despot and a torturer, and he has a tyrant's brutal cunning and twisted intelligence. He knows how to rule his minions with a rod of fear and they cower before him in terror as he howls with rage and gnashes his teeth and threatens them with ever more horrible punishments.

A cannibal, he will eat whatever is brought to him – be it Men, Dwarves, Elves, ponies or hobbits, and his cooks are forever attempting to create for him new and tempting recipes…

Orcs

Bigger, tougher and nastier even than their subterranean cousins, the Goblins, Orcs did not originate in Middle-earth as natural beings, but long, long ago were forged by agony and cruelty. For it is rumoured that once they were Elves, captured and tortured by an evil power until every good instinct towards beauty and nobility had been driven out of them. Thus reduced to hideous, vicious creatures, their only delight in life is to inflict pain and terror on others, as if to echo the torments their kind endured in a bygone age, even though no Orc honours or even owns that memory.

Living above ground, unlike the Goblins of the Misty Mountains, they are less stunted and diseased than their kin, although they too dislike the bright light of day, bred as they were in darkness. Armed with scavenged and remade weapons and in league with dark forces, they are ranging widely across Middle-earth, and are a deadly danger to travellers.

Where once they spoke the melodic Elven tongue, now, just as their faces and forms have been corrupted, so has the language they speak, tainted as it is with the Black Speech, an ugly mixture of guttural consonants and harsh snarls.

Wargs

Evil packs of giant wild wolves live on the borders of the unknown, under the shadow of the Goblin-infested Misty Mountains and over the Edge of the Wild. Their chief is a great white wolf, that rules over many hundreds of them, communicating both in howls and in the language of the Wargs, which is dreadful and cruel.

With their matted fur, blazing eyes and slathering jaws, they are a fearsome sight. But they are more fearsome by far if they are hunting, for they have a preternatural sense of smell and can run for miles and miles, more swiftly than a pony, even bearing Orcs on their backs.

They have entered into an unholy pact with the Orcs, frequently collaborating with them in evil deeds such as launching raids for plunder and slaves. The Orcs often ride them into battle; even though the Wargs have never been tamed, they offer their service of their own free and wicked will.

Radagast the Brown

The wizard Radagast is of the same Order as Gandalf the Grey, and his name in the ancient language of Adûnaic means 'tender of beasts'. Indeed, he prefers the company of animals, birds and trees to that of Men, wizards, hobbits, Dwarves, and even Elves. Spending most of his time in the wild, he examines the state of the world at close quarters, gathering plants and herbs for food and medicines, and communing with the forest.

He lives near the southern borders of the Greenwood (which some now call Mirkwood) in an extraordinary house called Rhosgobel, a ramshackle arrangement of stone and timber walls covered by a thatched roof. The house has been split in two by a huge oak tree that has been allowed to grow from an acorn. Being soft-hearted about all natural things, Radagast could not bear to uproot the tree, and so he has come to an accommodation with it, even though anyone else would find it extremely inconvenient to have to live around a tree.

Radagast can talk to birds and animals, and has greater understanding and wisdom than any other in Middle-earth in matters of animal and herb lore. Field mice have made a nest of his beard and all manner of birds land upon him to chirrup news into his ear. As a result his robes are always in the most frightful state, and his snaggle-toothed grin only adds to his curious appearance.

In times of great need he travels on a sleigh, which is pulled by eight pairs of enormous rabbits, and with this remarkable form of transport he can travel at great speed.

It is rare that he attends formal meetings with the other Istari wizards. His devotion to the wild things of Middle-earth has made him an unusual character and Saruman, for one, has nothing but contempt for his erratic ways. But Radagast should never be discounted as a fool, for although he is eccentric, he is still one of the Wise, with a sharply observant eye.

75

The Quest Continues...

To the east of the Misty Mountains, across the Great River Anduin, lies the huge forest of Mirkwood, once known as Greenwood the Great. Once it was a beautiful place but a sickness has fallen upon it and now it is wild and dark and full of dangers.

In order to reach the Lonely Mountain of Erebor, Bilbo Baggins and The Company must continue their perilous journey into this decaying, poisonous forest, in which unseen things rustle in the undergrowth and pale eyes stare out of the trees. Creatures of unspeakable evil now dwell in Mirkwood, and the ruler of this woodland realm bears a deep enmity for Thorin Oakenshield.

The way ahead will be fraught with all manner of life-threatening dangers. Surviving to reach their goal will require all the courage, determination and cunning that thirteen Dwarves and a single hobbit can muster.

HarperCollins*Publishers*
77–85 Fulham Palace Road,
Hammersmith, London W6 8JB
www.tolkien.co.uk

Published by HarperCollins*Publishers* 2012

1

ISBN 978-0-00-746795-2

Acknowledgements

There are a lot of people to thank for the making of this
Visual Companion – too many to mention every one of
them by name – but I would like to single out my agent
Jonathan Lloyd, editor Chris Smith and publisher David
Brawn; Natasha Hughes, Terence Caven, Ben Gardiner,
Andrew Cunning and Charles Light for their huge
efforts in putting the book together; the HarperCollins
rights and sales teams; at Warner Brothers Elaine
Piechowski, Victoria Selover, Melanie Swartz, Susannah
Scott and Jill Benscoter; in New Zealand Judy Alley,
Melissa Booth and Ceris Price, Alan Lee, John Howe,
Chris and Dan Hennah, and Matt Dravitzki; Richard
Taylor, Ann Maskrey and Brian Sibley for behind-
the-scenes information; and most importantly Peter
Jackson and the filmmakers for allowing me to make a
nuisance of myself on set, and the whole cast and crew
for invaluable insights into the characters and world of
The Hobbit.